George's New Dinosaur

George's favourite toy is Mr Dinosaur.

George likes bouncing Mr Dinosaur in the garden, playing with him at bath time, and he loves going to sleep with Mr Dinosaur beside him.

At bedtime Peppa says, "George, I think Mr Dinosaur is broken!"

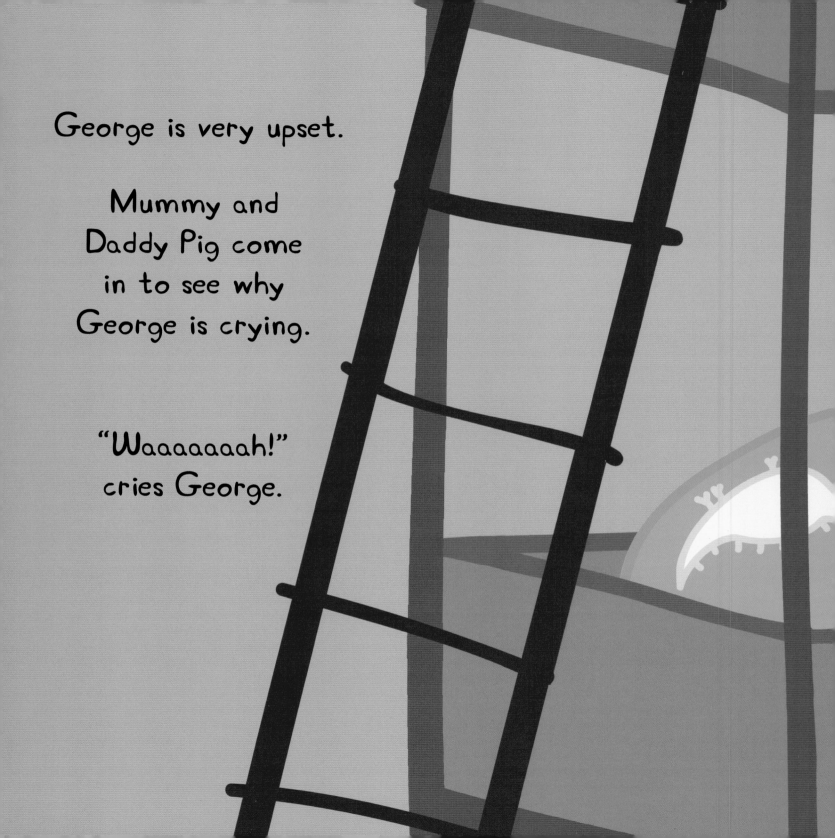

George is very upset.

Mummy and
Daddy Pig come
in to see why
George is crying.

"Waaaaaaah!"
cries George.

"Poor George," says Daddy Pig.
"Maybe it's time you got
a new dinosaur."

The next day, Peppa, George,
Mummy and Daddy Pig visit Mr Fox's shop.
"I'm sure we'll find a lovely dinosaur here, George!"
says Mummy Pig.
"Look, George!" says Daddy Pig pointing to
the shop window. "There's a big one!"
"Oooh dine-saw!" says George.

"Good morning!" beams Mr Fox. "Can I help you?"
"We'd like to buy the dinosaur in the window,
please," says Daddy Pig.
"Good choice!" says Mr Fox.
"This is Dino-Roar. He walks, he talks and he sings!"
"Wow!" says everyone.
"Dino-ROAR!" says George excitedly.
"We'll take it!" says Daddy Pig.

George is playing with Dino-Roar in the garden.
Dino-Roar sings,
"Dino-Roar, Dino-Roar!
Listen to Dino-Roar! Roooooaaaaaaaaar!"
"Careful, George," says Daddy Pig. "Don't play
too roughly because Dino-Roar will get broken."

George wants to play with Dino-Roar in the bath.

SPLASH,
SPLASH,

SPLASH!

"Dino-ROAR!" says George.
But Mummy Pig says, "George, if you get
Dino-Roar wet he'll stop working."

Peppa and George are
asleep in bed. But suddenly
Dino-Roar comes to life!

"ROAR! Dino-Roar,
Dino-Roar!"

"George!" says Peppa.
"Dino-Roar has
woken me up!"

"Maybe Dino-Roar should sleep
somewhere else," says Daddy Pig,
taking Dino-Roar away.

George is feeling sad. He cannot play with Dino-Roar in the garden, or the bath or even in bed.

"Never mind, George," says Mummy Pig brightly.
"Dino-Roar can still roar."
"Dino-Roar! Li . . . sten to Dino-Roo . . . aarr."
Dino-Roar stops walking and talking completely.

"I think the batteries must have run out,"
says Mummy Pig.

"Already? How many are there?" grumbles Daddy Pig,
as batteries pour out of Dino-Roar.
"Hundreds and thousands!" cries Peppa,
as she picks them up.

Peppa spots something green under a bush.
"What's this?" says Peppa. "Is it a trumpet?"
"You've found Mr Dinosaur's tail," says Mummy Pig.
"Now Daddy Pig can mend him."
"He might be a bit difficult to mend,"
says Daddy Pig doubtfully.

But the tail slips perfectly into place.
Daddy Pig has mended Mr Dinosaur.
"Ho ho ho," chuckles Daddy Pig.
"Hello, Mr Dinosaur," says Peppa.
"Grrrrr!" replies George.

"Hee hee hee!" everybody laughs.
Mr Dinosaur is George's favourite
toy in the whole world!